This book belongs to

....

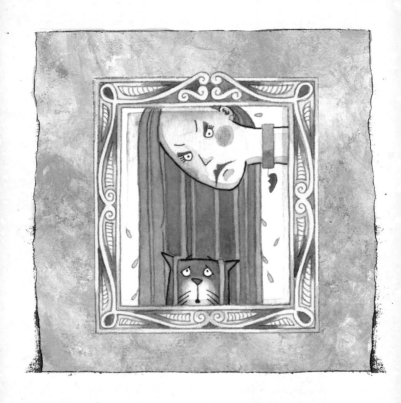

Snow White

Nick and Claire Page

Illustrations by Sara Baker

make
believe
ideas

Once there was a young princess with skin as white as snow, lips as red as blood, and hair as black as ebony. She was called Snow White.

Her mother was dead and her father had
married again. The new queen was beautiful
but vain. Every day she asked:
"Mirror, mirror on the wall,
who is the fairest of them all?"
And the mirror replied:
"You, O Queen, are the fairest, it's true,
No one else looks as good as you."

As each year passed, Snow White
grew more beautiful. One day, the
queen said to her mirror:
"Mirror, mirror on the wall,
who is the fairest of them all?"

The mirror answered:
"You, O Queen,
are a lovely sight,
but if you force
me to choose,
I'll go for Snow White."
The queen turned
yellow with shock,
then green
with envy.

So she ordered a huntsman to take Snow
White into the forest and kill her. But the
huntsman felt sorry for Snow White and
let her go. She ran through the forest,
until she came to a tiny house.

9

Inside, there was a table with seven places and seven little beds. Snow White lay on the beds and fell asleep.

Later, seven dwarfs came home from digging in the mines. They were surprised to find Snow White in their home!

10

"Who are you?" she asked.
"We are Monday, Tuesday,
Wednesday, Thursday, Friday,
Saturday, and Fred," they said.

The dwarfs agreed to let Snow White stay to
look after the house and cook their meals.

Back at the palace, the queen asked again:
"Mirror, mirror on the wall,
who is the fairest of them all?"

And the mirror replied:
"You, O Queen, have the beauty of night,
but you're still coming second to
Princess Snow White.
She's still alive and still good-looking.
She lives with the dwarfs and does
their cooking."

The Queen turned
purple with passion
and red with rage.

So, using her magic, she went to the
cottage, disguised as an old woman:
"Try my apples. Take a bite!
Just the thing for skin so white!"

Snow White didn't know it was the queen,
so she bought a juicy red apple. But the
apple was poisoned and when Snow White
took a bite, she fell down, as if dead.

The dwarfs found Snow White
lying on the ground.
"She's dead!" cried Monday,
Tuesday, Wednesday, Thursday,
Friday, Saturday, and Fred.

They put her in a glass coffin
and took turns to guard it.

The queen ran back to the palace.
"Mirror, mirror on the wall,
who is the fairest of them all?"

And the mirror replied, sadly:
"You, O Queen, are the fairest of fair.
Snow White's dead, so what do I care?"

One day, a prince came
riding through the forest
and saw Snow White lying
there, her skin as white as
snow, lips as red as blood,
and hair as black as ebony.
At once, he fell in love.
"Let me take her back to
my castle," he begged.
"I cannot live without her."

As his servants lifted the coffin, one tripped and the piece of poisoned apple fell out of Snow White's mouth.

At once, Snow White woke up!
"She's not dead!" cried Monday,
Tuesday, Wednesday, Thursday,
Friday, Saturday, and Fred.

Back at the castle, as usual, the
queen asked her mirror:
"Mirror, mirror on the wall,
Who is the fairest of them all?"
And the mirror answered:
"You, O Queen, are far from plain,
but Snow White is alive again!"

At this, the queen turned
every color under the sun,
all at once, until she shattered
into a thousand pieces.

So Snow White married the prince.
And the seven dwarfs came and saw
them every day: Monday, Tuesday,
Wednesday, Thursday, Friday,
Saturday, and Fred.

Ready to tell

Oh no! Some of the pictures from this story have been mixed up! Can you retell the story and point to each picture in the correct order?

27

Picture dictionary

Encourage your child to read these words from the story and gradually develop his or her basic vocabulary.

beautiful

disguised

dwarf

forest

mirror

palace

prince

princess

shattered

Key words

Here are some key words used in context. Help
your child to use other words from the border
in simple sentences.

Snow White **was** beautiful.

The queen did not **like** her.

The mirror **said** . . .

The prince saw Snow White.

They were happy.

Make a magic mirror

You may not be able to make a truly magic mirror,
but it's easy to make a mirror that's fit for a princess.

You will need

a mirror tile • sticky tape • a large sheet of cardboard
• a pencil • a ruler • paint or crayons • glue
• beads, feathers, toy jewels, and pieces of tissue paper

What to do

1 Take care! Some tiles have sharp edges. Ask a grown-up
to put tape around the edges to make them safe.
2 Carefully lay the tile on the middle
of the cardboard and draw around it.
3 Ask a grown-up to draw one line
about 1 inch (3 cm) outside the square,
and another 1/2 inch (1.5 cm) inside.
4 Cut along the two new lines to
make a simple frame. (You may
need a grown-up to help.)

frame

this part overlaps
the mirror

5 Color the cardboard, using crayons or paint (let it dry).
Stick beads, jewels, feathers, or bits of tissue paper on one
side of the frame. Make it look really special.
6 When the glue has dried, carefully stick the tile to the
back using strong tape.
Turn it over and you have a "magic" mirror of your own!